# WILDCLOWN HARD-BOILED

G. WELLS TAYLOR

Second Printing 2020

ISBN: 9798675312214

Cover design by G. Wells Taylor

# DEDICATION

For Wildclown Project Team Members:
**Richard Van Dyk and Robert A. Cotton**
Thanks.

# CONTENTS

# THE CAT LOVER

I don't like cats, so don't tell me that deep down, I do. And don't suggest that there was something wrong with my childhood. I didn't have one. I just don't like cats. They're not substantial enough for me.

If there's a dog in the room, you put your hand out and he'll put his head under it. But cats are like unfriendly ghosts. They appear out of nowhere, and then fall back into the shadows without a sound. I like to know when an animal's in the room with me—especially one that eats meat.

I have never liked cats, and I've grown close to hating them since the Change. Along with the resurrection of the dead, all animals, even our faithful dogs turned on us, left us to our fates, or worse attacked us outright. Feral pets have become a real problem, but none are more dangerous than the cat.

There have been attacks, many, and though they're rarely fatal, they maim, and disfigure. Greasetown Authority has a shoot on site rule for cats. But they move quickly, and you never hear them coming, suddenly you're bleeding and they're gone. Cat lovers say it's the Change, that whatever happened to the world, caused them all to go mad. Me, I think the cats have just been biding their time.

At least I never liked them so I've never felt betrayed.

A recent brush with success had left me with more money in my pocket than I owed. I even had some in the bank, so I decided to take a little holiday. A vacation was just what the doctor ordered.

It was Elmo, my business partner, who couldn't appreciate the finer aspects of rest and relaxation; and so, he obsessively answered the phone and accepted any business and made appointments with anyone who flashed a couple of hundred dollars our way. Like most dead people, Elmo's a workaholic.

I'd spent the last few months in and out of trouble, getting my chops busted, my head sapped and my shins bruised but I was working. I'm a detective and you have to take the jobs as they come; but success can kill in my business. Oh, in case you don't know, I dress like a clown. No fashion statement; it's a complicated deal I have worked out with the guy who owns the body I drive around in when I'm working. His name's Tommy Wildclown; but that's another story.

So, I knew that this kind of success would get me killed. If I didn't take some time off—I'd get sloppy and catch a bullet between the shoulder blades. As it was, my right wrist was broken, and bound up with a flexible plastic and plaster cast. It's what happens when a 200-pound man, that's me, punches a 400-pound man, that's the killer in my last case, in the forehead.

It didn't help that he was sitting down, and that his chair was braced up against the wall. I let him have it; actually I let the building have it, and knocked him out so fast he didn't hear me scream. So, some time off to nurse the wound.

To get it, I packed Elmo up and sent him on a luxury bus liner to Old Orleans to track down acquaintances and buy some sensible clothes. Fashion was Elmo's only weakness. I dropped him at the bus depot, and then hung around to wave goodbye. I halfway expected him to get off and hire me out to find missing luggage.

After the bus's taillights disappeared into the fog, I went to my favorite eatery to read newspapers and have the best breakfast a clown with a broken wrist could buy. Then, I bought the biggest and oldest bottle of Canadian Club whisky I could find.

My plan was to slip into a haze of delightful convalescence, talk to imaginary people, say what I'd like to say to people who pissed me off in the past, and maybe make a few crank phone calls.

I had a bag of groceries under one arm—man food, pickled stuff and pretzels, good for working up a thirst—plus my vintage whisky, as I fumbled inexpertly with the office key. I juggled my packages briefly, almost lost the jar of mustard, breathed a sigh of relief when the lock finally clicked, and pushed my way in.

I'd left the lamp on by the couch in the waiting room. Unable to move freely now, I pressed my groceries against my hip, and clutched the slippery bottle of Canadian Club in my armpit as my left hand stupidly tried to pull the key out of the lock. Feeling an avalanche building energy, I abandoned the key to limp as quickly as possible, contorting my body, to push the descending package outward, so it landed on the couch when it fell. That perilous situation dealt with, I turned back to the key—yanked it out, then shut the door.

I snatched up my bottle of whisky, passed quickly across the waiting room and into my office. There must have been something in the air, because I paused. *The window was open.* I had opened it to air the place out—if that was possible with the flatulent backwash Greasetown called air—but I had planned to shut it before taking Elmo to the bus station.

One thing you have to remember about the Change is you just don't leave your windows open. Things can get in—awful things. In a city that had a rising population of corpses walking its streets, you just don't leave your windows open. And there was the problem of animals hating people now. Even pigeons and sparrows had developed a hostile attitude—doves had become hawks.

I had only started to work into a good curse when I heard the growl. It was a bad one. Sort of the worst kind of growl you're going to hear in a nearly dark office. There is nothing like the sound of an angry cat—nothing at all. They produce an alien and monstrous noise, half growl, half wail. There doesn't seem to be a human analog to it.

I'm sort of stretching a point calling it a growl at all. It was a noise I'd expect to hear at the dawn of time, when there were just swamps and reptiles. And worst of all a cat only growls when he means business. I just had time to flip the light switch.

A high-pitched scream came with the light and a wiry black tangle of fur slightly bigger than a football hit my chest. I barely had time to get my left hand up. Needling pressure tore my skin, as the cat rocketed toward my face.

My arm deflected it. The cat scraped toward the elbow—its rear legs ripping at my gut. I swung the hand but the creature clung like a burr—fire leapt up my arm when it sank its fangs into my palm. On impulse, I flung the fist at the wall. Tightly wrapped around my whisky bottle it should have been a crushing blow, but the cat sensed the impact before it happened and tore up my arm toward my shoulder.

The Canadian Club thumped dully against the wall and bumped on the carpet when I released it. With my right hand, I clawed at my .44 automatic where it hung from my pink skipping rope belt. My fingers wrapped around it, but the cast had thickened my palm by an inch and I could not hook a finger around the trigger. Instead I whipped the weapon up and slapped the cat across the room with it.

I just managed to slip the gun into my left hand when the cat launched itself again. This time, I felt its claws dig into my scalp—felt them lacerate the skin around my right ear. I swung the gun at the cat again, and it leapt out of range, ran across the top of the door. I am not ambidextrous and have never made the claim. I try to be proficient in small arms fire with both hands, but bullets are expensive items, and I'm usually broke.

I fired the big gun, tore the top corner off my inner office door, fired again and killed a picture of a brewing company I kept over a small shelf of books. I fired again and mortally wounded my dictionary.

The cat bounded and bounced from shadow to shadow and landed on my desk yowling—cursing, I cradled the gun on my broken wrist and aimed at the cat as it sprung.

Cats do not do well against .44 caliber handguns when they're aimed properly—and even worse at a range of two yards. Evolution had not prepared them for this. And what was left of my feline attacker formed a red shrapnel cloud that littered my desk, and sent wads of black fur onto the wall behind it.

Somewhere in all that crashing, screaming violence the phone had started to ring. When the .44's roar subsided the bell was all I could hear.

I walked around the desk, still quaking with adrenaline. Pausing to flick the cat's tail off my chair, I forgot I wasn't going to answer the phone, and answered it.

"Hello," I said, surveying the bloody wreckage of my relaxing afternoon.

"I'm looking for Wildclown Investigations," came the voice, more clipped and officious than mine could ever be.

"You found it ..." I muttered, leaning forward to shove the black cat's lower jaw into the wastebasket. "I'm supposed to answer the phone with it."

"With what?"

"With *Wildclown Investigations*." I leaned back, and noticed a good quantity of blood up and down my arm. *Mine*, and there was a constant slow drip from the right side of my head. It pattered slowly onto my shoulder. Scalp wounds bleed like pigs. "How can I help you? I'm kind of busy."

"I would like to employ your services," said the voice.

"I'm on vacation," I said, dully aware of an ache in my knitting wrist.

"Then why did you answer your phone?"

"Okay you got me there." I cradled the blood-dappled receiver under my chin, reached into my pocket for a cigarette. Paused. "One moment," I said, snatching up the bottle of Canadian Club where it lay mercifully unbroken. I snatched off the seal, took a slug. Then resumed searching for my cigarettes until I found one and lit it. "How can I help you?"

"My name is Jonathan Kradzyk. I'm the curator of the Greasetown Metropolitan Museum of Antiquities." His voice really flowed around those words. I took another belt from my bottle as I listened. "And, well there's been trouble, strange trouble involving animals."

"Call the Humane Society." I watched a tuft of black fur waft toward the floor.

"It's more serious than that. It's one of our board members. Margaret Meadows of the Meadows Culinary Delights family." I knew the company. They made plankton and krill taste like hot dogs and hamburgers. "She's been killed at the museum."

"Call Authority."

"By CATS!" Mr. Kradzyk said, impossibly.

I paused to study the remains of a cat on my desk. "I'm all ears," I said, absently hoping I still had two.

"Can you come to the museum? I need this cleared up for our legal defense. In case her family suggests we bear any responsibility." He cleared his throat, uncomfortable. "I'm told that to protect ourselves we have to be sure there's nothing we could have done to prevent it."

"Sure, I'm on vacation. A trip to the museum fits." I knew the address, so just said two o'clock and hung up. Then I picked up the telephone book and looked through it for cleaning companies.

## 2

## Greasetown Metropolitan Museum of Antiquities

The Greasetown Metropolitan Museum of Antiquities is in the new section of town barely a stone's throw from its former haunt—a huge brownstone edifice that looked like it belonged in a museum. Its new digs were massive in their glassy prefabricated way, and boasted superior conditions for preserving the many artifacts contained therein.

The old building bordering the new part of town as it did was slated for the wrecking ball, as most things are, but had for the interim become a squatter's hotel for dead and living often drug-addicted indigents.

I made my way past the tall glass front doors of the new museum and into a foyer over which hung a massive mobile of cast iron. The sort of thing you knew some rich artist was laughing about somewhere, probably on the way to the bank.

I walked up to the front desk and met a man coming out of an office behind it. He had a fragile-boned, violin-playing look to him, wore a blond hairpiece and glasses. His suit was tailored and crisp and would have made Elmo envious. He paused when he saw me come in, then a smile spread over his meagerly fleshed face.

"Mr. Wildclown!" He followed his outstretched hand toward me. "I recognize you from the Gazette. The hearings ..."

"Yeah, I keep hearing about them." I shook the proffered hand with as much machismo as my cast would allow. "You're Kradzyk?"

"Oh, you've hurt yourself." His eyes did a study of the cast, and then whipped up to my face. The recent cat attack had not needed stitches to repair, but I was pretty sure that a couple of the wounds still oozed through my black and white clown's greasepaint.

"Shaving," I murmured looking around. "I'm all thumbs."

Kradzyk looked at me seriously a moment, then let go of the discussion with a grin. "I'm glad you could take time from your vacation to consult on this, Mr. Wildclown." His eyes looked inward. "Poor Margaret ..."

"Yeah ..." I leaned against the glass counter; my heavy shoulder inches away from pricey and delicate looking Aztec jewelry. "Fire away."

"We had a board meeting two nights ago, Wednesday. Just typical budget stuff." Kradzyk looked like he wanted to lean too but there wasn't room so he had to cross his arms. "Margaret was here with the other members. She was in charge of the African acquisitions committee. They put together purchase plans and accompanying cost sheets, it's all in an effort to keep the museum's collection interesting and exciting."

"Right." I was beginning to regret leaving the office. Still, the cleaners had left it stinking of ammonia, and there was no way I was going to air it out again. I lit up a cigarette.

Kradzyk paused to watch the blue smoke rise up into an air filter, a noticeable look of relief passed across his features and he continued. "The meeting ended at ten o'clock. I locked up and the next morning, she was found by our cleaning staff, dead in the Egyptian artifacts wing."

"Where?" I asked. It was a toss up, say that or ask for a drink. So, I followed Kradzyk through dimly lit hallways past ancient arts and crafts until we passed under a sign that said: *Egypt Land of Mystery.*

Inside, there were numerous glass cases housing ancient fabric and jewelry. There was a mummy—evidently missing the strange 'undead' animation that most of the dead had been endowed with since the Change. I'd read about the problem with mummies.

Most had had their brains sucked out as part of the mummification process. And the brain was important to the living death that the dead could enjoy with the Change. Drying out for a couple of thousand years didn't help either. A mummy wouldn't be able to move if he wanted to.

"You say she was killed by cats," I said as Kradzyk came to a halt beside a large stone sculpture—a man's body about ten feet tall with a cat's head. "What happened after Blacktime? What did she say?" I was referring to the time that the dead experienced between living and reanimation.

"The cats ate her tongue and lips, eyes—her whole face." Kradzyk looked nauseous shaking his head. "There's some doubt that she will regain her sanity. And it may be for the best."

I looked up at the sculpture and felt my hackles rise at the inscrutable cat's face carved there. "Ironic." I looked down the length of the sculpture to the section of concrete beneath my feet where the bloodied carpet had been cut away. "The cats killed her here?" I gestured at the sculpture. "In front of him."

"Oh, that has been a subject of some discussion I assure you." He dipped his chin at the cat-person sculpture. "*Bast*, that's the Egyptian Cat god. Supposedly a friendly incarnation of the lioness goddess, Semha, Skemet ... her name escapes me. Not my specialty." The curator shook his head. "Authority forensics took up that section of carpet and is supposed to be investigating the death, but I was surprised that it did not provoke a stronger response from them."

"Authority's got its own troubles right now." And that was true, since the infighting started; they'd been busier investigating each other than the populace. It was part of the reason my business had suddenly boomed. People needed help and Authority couldn't give it right now. "Why do you think it was cats?"

Kradzyk frowned. "The type and number of injuries, the extent of the trauma to the body and well, in the blood, we found paw prints. Many prints."

"But no cats."

"No," he said and smiled. "Why do you say that?"

"You wouldn't need me then. You could explain it as a freak accident caused by an open window or vent. Cats don't like people anymore, remember?" I dropped my cigarette butt on the concrete and ground it out beneath my boot.

"Well," Kradzyk said, motioned toward a vent in the wall, "One of the investigating inspectors pointed to that. The casing *was* off that morning. The investigator said that there has been a sharp increase in the feral cat population in town. They're after the rats ..." I walked over and inspected the four-by-eight-inch grate while the curator talked to my back. "But that's ridiculous. To imagine the cats came in through that—enough to kill a woman."

"That goes to an air exchanger?" I ran a hand up the wall as I stood.

"Yes. Which makes it completely ridiculous." Kradzyk took a step away, momentarily unsettled by my clown detective shtick. "We checked the air exchanger on the roof that day. All of its vents were screwed into place."

"That's good." I walked back toward the stone cat goddess. "If she was killed here, it wasn't by cats. But she probably wasn't killed here."

"Why would you say that?" Kradzyk looked pleasantly surprised.

"Well because then I'd have to suggest that a group of cats were acting in concert. Either they had a key to the building, or a screwdriver, knew Mrs. Meadows was here, waited for the meeting to end, let themselves in and killed her so fast that there is no evidence of a fight." I remembered my own tangle with the cat that morning.

"Of course," Kradzyk groaned, looking mildly chastised.

"What was her committee working on?"

"Oh, many things. She was in the process of acquiring a large Moroccan collection from the City of Light's Museum of Culture and Technology. Some sort of trade she was working out." He looked deflated, studying the stone sculpture.

"All seems silly now," he said staring at me evenly, a slight tremor of embarrassment flexing beneath his features. He pointed to my head. "You're bleeding."

"Oh ..." I wiped at the blood with my hand, saw Mr. Kradzyk nod. "It's two hundred dollars a day. I'd like to talk to Mr. Meadows. There *is* a Mr. Meadows, isn't there?"

"Yes. Mr. Meadows was a board member before Margaret was. But he quit. Actually he looked after the same African Acquisitions committee. I don't know what his reasons were for leaving. I just know that before Mrs. Meadows took over the job, things had stagnated."

"So." I looked at our stone friend and the other exhibits. "He was responsible for acquiring these pieces?"

"The older ones." Kradzyk looked up at Bast. "I believe."

I looked up at Bast's big cat face, and then turned to Kradzyk. "Can I get his phone number?"

"Certainly." Mr. Kradzyk's eyes lingered on my bleeding head and then retreated. I followed slowly feeling in need of restoration.

# 3
## The Meadows Place

Making seafood taste like ballpark franks seemed to have paid off for the Meadows family. They owned part of a spacious living complex called Glade Tidings on the west side of Greasetown.

The complex was designed to resemble a massive estate in the English countryside—crushed gravel driveway, the works. It was divided into four complete castles connected by a central recreation facility. A tall stone wall protected the perimeter.

I had to pick up a pass at the guardhouse to get through the gates—a side effect of the walking dead and rising crime rate that came with the Change.

The house or condominium or semi-detached mansions shared the large tree-covered grounds. I had heard there was a manmade lake out there somewhere and pondered setting a hook for a manmade fish.

I pulled up to the front of the manor house and climbed out of the car. I was driving a retro-Galaxy 2000 called a Galaxy XM. Elmo had picked it out himself since he did most of the driving. I chose the black paint over the dark green he was toying with.

Walking toward the house, I slipped a hand along my belt, and patted the gun that nestled there. My compromise with Tommy, wherever his spirit lurked in the shadows of my borrowed body, had allowed the fairly recent addition of an overcoat and fedora to the drably painted clown's coverall.

It was a welcome change with Greasetown's meteorologists calling for rain slightly more than 95 percent of the time.

I had found, in the last six months or so that Tommy's psyche had become more and more cooperative. I had my moments—certain things still set him off, and I was occasionally forced to struggle for the steering wheel; but I found that the odd night I was able to sleep in the body as well.

There were still times I relinquished control for no other reason than I did my best thinking when disembodied.

It was Saturday, around eight. I had called ahead, and caught Mr. Meadows at home. I told him I was a detective hired by the museum. It was just a formality, but I had to ask him a few questions about his wife. He agreed, be there around eight.

My boots crunched on the wet gravel as I approached the flagstone walkway. At the door, I paused for a final drag from my cigarette, pitched the damp butt into the garden and knocked.

The door swung wide. There was a gentleman, must have been sixty pre-Change years of age. All the extra years that the Change's longevity gave to the living weighed heavily upon him. There were creases on his face that were deep enough to lose a quarter in. Then I remembered; his wife had just died. I took off my hat as his expression gave away his surprise.

"Why, are you? You are? I've, I've heard about you." He pointed a finger. "*Read* about you."

"Wildclown, pleased to meet you Mr. Meadows. I'm sorry about your wife." I could see him racing toward the question about the makeup so I cut him off at the pass.

"I'd like to ask you a few questions about Mrs. Meadows." I gave him my strictly business face. "I have a Photostat of my license if you prefer."

"No, Mr. Wildclown." He stepped back pulling the door wide. "I was startled. That's all. But it's come back to me. The newspaper stories—about the *Death House*. Forgive me."

"No need to apologize Mr. Meadows." I walked into the foyer and was immediately impressed. Why not, it was designed that way. There was a massive cherry wood staircase that swept up in front of me. It led to an open pillared walkway upstairs of the same construction punctuated with many doors.

Under this, to each side of the stairs, a room opened outward that looked like it had hosted King Arthur and the round table knights in another life. A huge fireplace ringed round by heavy wooden furniture was at the far end of it. Shelves on the walls held hundreds of books, there were coats of arms on plaques, and guarding numerous dark alcoves were authentic-looking suits of armor.

"Please come in." He stepped aside but kept his hands out for my hat and coat. I made no move to give them to him so he simply nodded. "Do come in. Please." And he started away from me toward the fireplace talking over his shoulder. "My serving staff is away. I—I wanted to be alone with my thoughts and so many of them were devastated by Margaret's death."

"Of course." I moved to the warmth of the fireplace, stood in front of it looking at the flame.

"Can I offer you a drink?" Meadows said to my back.

"I'll take a whisky or scotch." I had the urge to kick at the logs in the fire. "Please."

I turned in time to see his broad backside move toward a liquor stand and tray that was on wheels, parked close to a chair with an open book on it, beside a floor lamp. That would be handy in a big place like this, the liquor on wheels—might even be good for the office.

Mr. Meadows returned now with a hefty drink in each hand—the kind of *hefty* that would take the edge off the day. Meadows' hair and eyes were the same faded gray. His smoking jacket looked drained of color too.

"You share your wife's interests." I took the glass and a quick bolt of scotch: sweet and malty.

"I'm sorry?" Meadows' gaze followed mine to the book on his chair.

"*Sehkmet.*" My voice echoed in the glass. "Egyptian isn't it?" The title of the book was *The Legends of Sehkmet.* I tried to remember the name Kradzyk had stumbled over.

"Oh, oh, the book." He shook his head. "I'm a hobbyist, truly. I turn an eye to it, fascinating. Though my interest is of a more philosophical nature."

"*Philosophical.*" I felt the fire's heat on my back. "And *Bast.* Isn't this Sehkmet related to Bast somehow? Do you know anything about Bast?" I was just starting into a discussion with him, but something in the way he'd taken my interest in Sehkmet made me want to taunt him with *Bast.* "The curator, Mr. Kradzyk, at the museum, I believe he referred to *Sehkmet* as we spoke about *Bast.*"

"What about Bast?" His eyes had narrowed and his voice held a hesitant quality.

"You didn't like your wife's work did you, Mr. Meadows?" I dribbled the last of my drink onto my tongue. I was sure it would be impolite to ask for another so soon and resisted the urge to hold the empty glass out.

"What do you mean?" Meadows was doing a good job of looking aghast, and I began to doubt my line of questioning. He continued, "I held the same position myself."

"Terrible isn't it. The way it happened." I couldn't resist and kicked one of the burning logs now. A geyser of orange sparks shot up.

"It is." Turning to him, I could see that the question calmed him a little. "I assumed that was what you were here to talk to me about."

"It is." I ran a finger along the marble mantle. "It's all ironic."

"Yes it is." Mr. Meadows' shadow grew up beside mine. "She loved cats."

This time it was my turn to look aghast. I couldn't help but run that sad story from start to finish. Imagining a cat lover dying in such a way. Torn to pieces. *Cat got your tongue?*

"I'm afraid it is only half her problem." Meadows turned away. I watched him from the corner of my eye. "She is dead, with specialists now;

but her afterlife will be terrible. Disfigured as she is. Her mind was broken by the attack. They think she came out of Blacktime before the cats were finished."

I imagined the scene until it started to penetrate the edge of the scotch's growing numbness. "Did it bother you that she was about to trade away the collection that you had worked so hard to acquire?"

Mr. Meadows stepped up to me—an angry look crossed his features and was gone without a trace. "That's ridiculous. I relinquished *my* position on the board." He reached out for my glass. "Refill?"

I looked down, and then nodded. "Always."

"So you are saying what?" Meadows walked back to his liquor wagon and I listened to him pour.

"You left the museum. Kradzyk said that the African collection had stagnated during your tenure." I watched him flinch a little at that.

"I acquired some magnificent pieces for the museum." His voice had a hard edge this time. "I don't call that stagnation." He turned with the drinks and came toward me. "You should have seen it before I took the position. Spears, shields, a few masks. It lacked depth. It was devoid of meaning."

"I see," I said watching his face. There was no fear there. just sadness. "Then it would be difficult to see your work traded away."

"That is the nature of a museum. The bartering of exhibits often facilitates the acquisition of new pieces. Museums are under-funded, that's how it works." He held my drink out to me. "What do you propose? That I somehow conjured cats to kill my wife, and then wiped them away with a wave of my hand. All because I did not want her to undo the work I had accomplished in a volunteer capacity at the local museum?"

I took the drink, set my lips to it and as I did our eyes locked. We paused both of us eye to eye for a minute until Meadows' face cracked in a grin. He started laughing and a second later I was on the verge of embarrassment.

"No," I said, finally, took a seat across from Mr. Meadows. "I'm not saying that." I took another good haul from my drink. "I'm not sure what to think of it. A woman killed by cats, impossibly. But with the Change making all animals hate people, I don't know why I'd need a motive. I just have to find out how they got in and how they got out."

"The world has Changed." Meadows sat down, took a drink from his glass and watched the fire. "It has changed. And I told Margaret as much. The changes had to be respected. People must see this."

"Well, she kept busy. Involved in the community." I was beginning to like the hazy glow around the fire—downright vacation-like. "She adapted. Why did you quit the museum?"

"Because they did not understand the value of what they were acquiring. What they were doing." Meadows shook his head. "I did not think that it would be Margaret—my replacement. But she excelled in her position and began to think the way *they* think."

"You don't sound happy about that." I pointed impolitely.

"I wasn't happy. No." A dark pall fell across his features. "I had no idea she would take my position."

"So it did bother you that she was undoing your work."

"If they didn't have the right, why would she?" His eyes looked inward, searching. "They were not sanctified for Sehkmet."

"How's that?" Definitely now, I could see an aura around the flames. A little panic started at the back of my mind but something kept me from moving. "Sanctified?"

"They would handle artifacts from which magical powers bled, that in ages past had been filled with human life essence, human souls ..." His eyes did not meet mine. I could only see shadows. "To call them mere acquisitions! No human may acquire or possess these things—it is sacrilege. But only did they see the value, the commercial value. I would not participate. And then Margaret took the position. I tried to dissuade her."

Now I could definitely tell that something was up. My tongue felt all leathery. The way it feels after a whole bottle of whisky not two drinks. And my sinuses were drying out on top of my rapidly depleted vision ... I tried to get to my feet, and collapsed on the floor.

"It was everything I could do to forestall the trade ... but to no effect." The last thing I remember was Meadows standing over me. There was something about his eyes, something feral, like the cat I'd shot that morning. "These things are sacred. And the time for respect is at hand."

# 4
## Sehkmet

Lucky for me, years of heavy drinking had made me a very expensive date, and whatever Mr. Meadows had slipped into my glass along with the excellent scotch whisky was not enough to keep me out for long.

I awoke in darkness, luckily again, still in possession of Tommy's body. My vision was shot, and somewhere there was a distant ache from my far right hand that I knew would eventually make its way home to me, to pleasure my nights with excruciating pain.

*If I survived.* I flexed my arms and they were numb—tied at the wrists with coarse rope and bolted to some kind of setting overhead. The air was cool and damp around me.

Sadly, my nose was not similarly desensitized, and the sheer ammonia fire that registered almost knocked me out again. It smelled like I was on the shores of a great lake of cat urine. The foul air scoured my eyes, scorched my nostrils. My skin crawled at its touch.

I paused, mid-vomit to watch a dark-robed man with a torch walk down a spiral iron stair. I was in some kind of spacious cavern. In the new light, I could see that I was in a natural cave of slate-like rock that produced odd reflected angles. I knew instinctively that the spiral stair would lead up to the Meadows house, probably the basement. The cavern consisted of the same material that made up the bedrock for Greasetown and a long section of coast.

Mr. Meadows continued down the stair then stopped at the bottom. His torch, it turned out was some kind of gas lamp. It threw a lot of light around the cavern and illuminated two things: thirty feet in front of me stood the massive stone sculpture of Bast that I'd seen at the museum, and in front of that, a roughly circular pit about fifteen feet across. *Three things*, an altar sat at its edge in front of Bast. From the dark pit came a quiet rustling punctuated by low growls.

Meadows walked over to the altar and set the lamp down. He bowed to the sculpture mumbling in an alien language before making his way to me.

"So, you've just lost your mind then?" I said. My tongue had awakened enough by now. "Sure makes my job easier."

Meadows' serene expression flashed ire as he slapped me hard across the face. All of my old injuries fired on that one. "Silence!"

So, I watched him for a few seconds, as I focused on my legs' unchained status. I gauged the distance between Meadows' face and my boots.

"You do not understand!" Meadows hissed and walked away.

"Your wife was going to trade away the fake statue of Bast that you put at the museum," I said as Meadows whirled glaring. "I've got a bad feeling for the guy who carved it."

"This is Sehkmet!" The madman turned back to the statue, fell to his knees and bowed low. "She has come to revenge her many injuries. Now she will not wear the soft fur of companionship. She comes to slay her betrayers."

"Sehkmet," I said quietly. "*She's* coming?"

"She is here. As the other old gods have come." He rose to his feet, came toward me. "That is why the animals of the earth have chosen this time to slay us as they can."

"And you've decided to help." I tested my legs, quietly put weight on my toes. "Your wife was trading away the sculpture. Your forgery would be discovered, and your 'church' here would be exposed. What do you guys do meet Fridays? Bingo on Mondays?" I saw anger flash in his eyes. "So, you brought her here, tied her up, and fed her to your cats."

"Not for me. For Sehkmet." He walked behind me. I turned my head and saw him tugging at the rope. A pulley on the ceiling would pick me up and lower me into the hole in front of Sehkmet.

"Your cats are in the pit?"

"They are not *my* cats!" he hissed in my ear. "They are incarnations of Apocalypse. As the demons return to the world for vengeance their servants prepare the way. The loyal may serve them in the New Age."

"Sure," I said, certain that my legs would cooperate when I needed to do something. "And your wife was a sacrifice. As I bet your accomplices were who helped you bring Sehkmet here." I gestured to the idol with my chin. "Your accomplices, I can understand. Probably members of your church, or maybe just some paid workers right? Maybe they were dead already. But your wife. Was she unconscious when you killed her, or did you like it when she screamed?"

I took a hard hit in the back of the head this time, but the action slackened up the rope in Meadows' hands, and allowed me to fall forward.

I had to move quickly, and started to run, immediately feeling the rope begin to tighten as Meadows realized his mistake. Then it went taut, but not before I could take one good bound that sent me pivoting upward over the pit in front of the statue.

Meadows pulled again, which brought me arcing upward enough to deliver the stone statue of Sehkmet a hard double kick to the face.

That brought a scream from Meadows, who released the rope. And I was falling toward the crevasse full of cats. For a glimmering second I saw the multi-colored blanket of death, their incandescent eyes.

I jammed both elbows hard into the slate at the pit's edge, and struggled against the jarring action as my legs slapped the sheer side of the chasm. A great chorus of cat growls rose to greet me. Hands tied, and heavy rope sliding past me, I knew that I'd be pulled in as the last played out.

There was a heavy hollow knocking sound in the background and I realized that my kick had unbalanced the statue. I heard Meadows shrieking, running toward the idol.

Suddenly sharp white pain lanced up my leg as a cat made the leap and sunk its claws and teeth. Adrenaline flooded through me, and I crushed it against the cliff wall with my knee—its ribcage collapsed—then I scrambled up as another cat leapt onto my back.

I rolled onto the starving blood-mad creature turning in time to see Meadows run to Sehkmet's statue hands out before him.

As I elbowed a cat to death, I watched the statue continue its rocking motion—perhaps it wouldn't have tipped if he hadn't pushed back.

A scream and crushing sound. And the statue collapsed on Meadows.

He tried to get out of the way; he probably should have taken the full hit to end it quickly. Instead, the statue caught his foot, crushing it into place while his body hung over and into the pit.

Meadows screamed when he realized his peril; it must have been something looking down at all those hungry cats. And then he was covered in a rending cloud of carnivores. I saw his free leg kick outward feebly, and his arms flail briefly.

There was nothing I could do short of amputating his leg to pull him out. I briefly toyed with the idea of finding my gun and putting him out of his clawing, screeching misery. Then I remembered what he had planned for me.

I took the spiral stairs upward in search of a phone.

# 5
## A Time Coming

I made my way to the desk at my office. Sat down. The ammonia from the cleaners was like fresh flowers after the nostril scorching I'd received from the cat urine. I poured myself a drink and stretched back in my chair—my eyes dully scanned the outer world through the blinds.

It was five a.m. and I was going to drink myself silly. If I were lucky, I'd stagger into the outer office and slip into a coma round about the time that people used to go to church.

Authority had arrived at the Meadows' place pretty promptly after my call, all things considered, and thanked me for the help in their ungrateful way, before debriefing and ordering me off the premises. They were going to use some kind of carbon monoxide machine to kill all the hungry kitties Meadows kept in his basement before they burned them.

Meadows had been going nuts over the past couple of years and it was the primary reason he had abandoned his place on the museum board of directors. Sadly, no one but his wife knew about his new cat obsession. She had quietly covered for his hobby of collecting and trapping the felines for preservation in his secret basement.

Margaret Meadows took the job on the board to extend her protection of his madness, but had no idea how lethal his obsession had become. When her plans to trade the statue threatened to expose Meadows' Sehkmet religion and theft, he had decided to act. Evidently, he killed her at home after her last board meeting in his little secret sanctuary before bringing the body to the museum.

She had indeed planned to trade the statue of Sehkmet to the museum in the City of Light and they might recognize the forgery.

The recent Authority infighting could have made him confident enough to kill her for her sins. They wouldn't likely investigate something that was clearly the work of animals.

On a hunch, I'd asked about access to the old museum, and it turned out there was a service tunnel that was used for transporting relics during the move and then boarded up. Meadows had brought his wife's body into the museum that way, and left her.

Being a touch insane and a religious zealot, he'd left her body by the statue of Sehkmet as a warning, adopting the air of the educated that a dumb flatfoot would never make the connection or a detective in clown's greasepaint.

Kradzyk paid me four hundred dollars and put a lot of emphasis on me not making a big deal of it with the press. No one could explain the paw prints on the piece of carpet around Margaret Meadows' body and Kradzyk explained that Authority forensics had since lost track of the evidence.

As I sank slowly into drunken silence I wondered about the madman's predictions. Maybe there was a time coming when we would learn respect.

## DROP DEAD BLONDE

Christmas after the Change is the evil twin to its pre-Apocalyptic counterpart, I'm told. See, I don't remember much about the world before. Things have changed for me too. My particular brand of amnesia leaves me playing mental leapfrog with a madman that dresses like a clown and seems to have memory troubles of his own.

But that's all beside the point, another story—the icing on *my* cake. It left me here at a bar with a drink in the hand of a borrowed body contemplating Christmas in a world without children while a dead man noisily slurped a martini two stools down. At least I had a drink in hand. Oh, and a cigarette too. I'm always smoking.

I celebrated the season that way bellying up to a bar at my least favorite drinking establishment, and pounding down one whisky after another until I was able to look at the world without wincing.

People still gave each other presents, the churches sent out carolers and staged second-rate reenactments of the Greatest Story Ever Told but it didn't go much farther than that. Everyone was going through the motions.

The Change woke us from dreams of sugar plum fairies and coldly squelched all thoughts of salvation. The walking dead, constant rain and Greasetown's recurring blackouts didn't help either. It was hard to celebrate giving and taking in an endless downpour without the traditional flashing lights and ornaments while the cold eyes of the dead watched you from the shadows.

Authority restricted power usage to one hour a day per household or company for nonessential energy requirements during the Yuletide. People complained at first, but there were no longer any children, so what was the point.

Just after the Change, when we realized that the human race had become sterile, but before we understood that the children who remained were not going to grow up—people rallied around their Christmas trees like an antithesis of despair. But as time pressed on and children physically remained children, people realized that yet another terrible thing had happened

Somehow, the knowledge that their minds continued to mature in the stunted bodies made the horror of their situation all the more unimaginable.

Soon after that realization, Authority rounded up all the forever children they could find promising the public it was for protection and study. Many parents escaped the edict by running inland with their children only to disappear in the lawless wilderness that was growing there.

Stories circulated about a place in the forests where the forever children ran free, but a few days in Greasetown under the Change would make you realize how hollow that sounded. Some still remained in the cities—these children who would not age—but they were rare and had suffered much worse than Authority scrutiny. Most had fallen into the grips of unscrupulous men who ran the sex trade.

I managed to avoid despair by working and drinking hard—not always in that order and rarely exclusive of each other.

I'm a detective.

I'd like to say I was just sitting there minding my own business. I was in a way, being about three-quarters involved in bobbing for ice cubes in a potent Rusty Nail. December twenty-fourth had been a long day, and I needed something with a little extra kick that wouldn't knock my teeth out.

The drink was prepared for me by a stocky lady barkeep with a large droopy belly that completely smothered the dirty apron that struggled to peek out from beneath it. As I mentioned my attention was not altogether focused on my drink and the lady who served it.

For the last few minutes my mind had been drawn from its quiet pickling to the ragged couple down the way, just past the dead guy drooling gin. They were an awful looking pair of bar flies that had been buzzing over an escalating series of arguments. He had just threatened to slap her face, an action that one look told me would produce a dustbowl of pancake powder.

Not much of a threat since the man appeared to have reduced himself to a level where he'd have a tough time knocking the dandruff off his shoulders. But as my blood alcohol level rose, I had a growing sense of compassion for the woman—if for no other reason than for her eyes that seemed lost and homesick behind a tall stand of false eyelashes.

It's a sobriety test for me. As soon as I begin to sympathize with the other boozehounds at the bar, I knew it was time for a sensible man to go home.

Maybe it was Christmas, maybe it was the half-bottle of scotch I'd swallowed in the car, but I had just decided to down my last innocent bystander's drink and play cop when a voice spoke over my shoulder.

"I can't believe some people," it said, simple, husky and full of self-assurance.

I turned to look at the owner and almost dropped my chin in the ashtray.

The first thing that grabbed a hold of my tongue was a pair of pale blue eyes that seemed to glow with an inner light. The pupils were utter blackness and appeared to float in hazy azure pools. The eyes were enough to hold me stupid, blinking in reply; but finally a flash of her pale lashes introduced me to the rest of her face.

Framed in a cascade of blonde, brown and frosty curls to the shoulder, the face held a light sandy hue—made tantalizingly youthful by a spray of small pale freckles. The eyes sat under a narrow forehead on either side of a thin, straight nose. Full lips pulled back in a smile revealing straight white teeth that said without speaking: *I know you want me.*

And they were right. My first impulse was to bare my throat to them.

A quick peek at her body, a rapid, very urbane and sophisticated glance showed me a sleek and well-muscled form wrapped in a black skin-tight shirt and slacks. The neon red from a beer sign over the bar gave her whole body a purplish passionate glow. I counted her nipples out of the corner of my eye. Two: my favorite. She tossed her leather jacket on a barstool and climbed aboard.

Then her smile tightened and a deliciously goofy grin slid over her features. "Earth to the guy in clown makeup! Can you read me? Over?" She laughed and slapped a forearm I had left on the bar. The eyes flashed by me, and then happily hovered over the unhappy couple. "Looks like they made up."

I turned to watch the barflies kissing awkwardly as they left the bar arm in arm.

"Thank God they can't reproduce," she said.

"Every day," I countered, suddenly stumbling upon my voice box.

"Erin Moore," the blonde said, her eyes mercilessly gripping mine.

"Wildclown." I smiled flatly; gesturing at my face paint as I shook her small soft hand, hoping it would be enough. I found explaining the clown face the hardest part. It was embarrassing and Tommy, my host, tended to start to rail with indignation wherever he lurked during my possessions.

"I noticed." Her teeth paused, point to point. "It's *wild* clown."

"I was just having a drink," I said as I felt the first pang of Tommy's annoyance. I had to move quickly or risk being expelled from the body. Then I'd be forced to watch Tommy take over and screw up the introductions from where I hovered near the ceiling when disembodied. "I was wondering if you wanted one."

"I do want one." She looked away and scanned the labels on the spigots. "Something big and brown."

I bought a round and started a long evening of great stories and interesting opinions. We didn't even talk about Christmas more than once or twice. Like me, Erin knew there was no reason to talk about the ghost of a holiday. And the more she talked, the more I realized she had a way of making me forget who I was, where I was and what I did for a living. Her voice chatted and laughed me far from the world of the Change, to some sort of a place of memory approaching sunny.

I couldn't believe it, but decided to let myself. And her eyes, they pulled me easily longingly toward a place I'd almost forgotten about. I let myself go a little. Stupidly.

She had been a nursery school teacher before the Change, and had worked for a while with forever children in the years just following it, before Authority had started the big round up. Later courses in narrative psychology bought her a profession doing motivational lectures for corporations.

I took her avoidance of my makeup story as her polite and sensitive nature when I should have taken it as a warning. I'm just over six feet tall and about two hundred pounds. My face is decorated like a clown's in black and white; a thin skipping rope belt around my spotted coverall holds a powerful handgun. *I* would have asked.

By the end of the night I was ready to do anything for this mysterious former nursery school teacher; I'd fallen under her enchantment. Much later, when I returned from the little clown's room I discovered she was gone. The barkeep grunted at my unspoken query and gestured to the door. I looked out through the hazy glass and watched gray slush slowly piling up in the street. A car went by with a noisy hiss.

I returned to the bar and spent a somber hour recovering my inebriation sipping a pair of triple scotches. Erin Moore was an interesting woman. I was lucky to have met her in the first place. One final glare at the bartender, I paid, struggled into my overcoat and left.

# 2
## Fu Manchu and Blackbeard's Ghost

Fumbling at my office door I had a slight grin under my clown's smile. Life was too hard in Greasetown in the world after the Change to look any gift horse in the mouth. And Erin Moore was just that. She was the extent of my Christmas, and she had transported me to a time outside the rainy cold and damp. I had to smile. It would make hating the days to come that much easier.

A pair of sturdy hands on my shoulders swung me around so that a second pair, these curled into knobby fists worked my stomach just long enough to knock my gun to the floor and the breath out of my lungs. I dropped to my knees and dragged a painful bite of air over my teeth.

All four hands grabbed me this time, hoisted me into the air and slammed me against the doorframe hard enough to crack the window. Distantly I noticed the thin line trace through the last 'n' in 'Investigations' and the 'ld' in 'Wildclown.' My dead sidekick Elmo would have had a kitten over that one. He loved that window.

But his feline distemper would have to wait. I couldn't expect him back until the end of the week. He was over in Gritburg visiting a living relative from the south. Christmas right ... Like most dead people, Elmo suffered some long-term memory loss. He had been able to recover some of it after a visit to Old Orleans where he had lived his life as a private investigator before the Change and his death. Family he found told him he was Baptist.

The two thugs who had worked me over and were now crushing me against the doorframe appeared to have skipped science class the day they were discussing evolution. Both were wide-framed and heavy-featured and would be more at home in animal skins than in the tailored wool suits and overcoats they wore. Their dark fedoras obscured their faces with shadow.

One threw an arm across my throat and leaned in. Closer inspection showed me that he had a long droopy mustache like Fu Manchu. His breath stank of cigarettes and neglect. He lodged me firmly into place while his comrade, this one's outstanding feature was a black bristly beard, went through my pockets with his thick fingers.

"Hey!" he growled. Malicious joy filled his features and revealed large crooked teeth. "What's this?" He drew his hand from my pocket. In it was a large white envelope folded in half. I'd never seen it before. I smiled as he held it up.

"You're in for it now!" said Fu Manchu and his grip on me slackened for a second—not quite long enough for me to overpower them and escape, but just enough time for him to pull a pistol or lead sap out of his pocket and dent my skull with it.

As I dropped into darkness I heard someone laughing.

## 3
## The Boss

As I have done on an occasion or two before, I awoke tied to a chair. It was dark and I was still in possession of the, *my* body. I say that because in the past, such loss of consciousness usually accompanied my immediate rejection by my host. The throb in my right temple told me that I was still in charge and sobering up at an alarming rate.

A rope expertly bound my hands at the wrists to the rungs in the back of the chair, and another pliant piece of nylon raced around my chest about thirty times. My legs and feet were unbound but I didn't feel like going anywhere anyway, so I just sat there.

The smell of damp was the room's most distinguishing characteristic. A musty heavy quality hung in the air and made shallow breathing most comfortable. I detected the scent of cigarette smoke and warily glanced around for the dimensions of my prison. I finished quickly.

The room was constructed of flat limestone bricks piled eight feet high and about twenty-five feet on a side. There was an old wooden door covered with chipped red paint on my right and a small dirty sink and washstand against the wall on my left. I knew there was a dim lamp behind me because the wall opposite was black with my huddled shadow.

The red door opened. Fu Manchu entered followed by Blackbeard a second later. A third person appeared at the door but paused a moment backlit by the glare from the outer hall. He was about my height and width. His well-tailored suit did not obscure the fact that he had a slimmer build, angular. And he moved with crisp practiced motions. With a continuous sweep of his arms he lit a cigarette he had procured from a case deftly pulled from an overcoat pocket and replaced. Smoke blew from his nostrils in thin, straight lines.

Fu Manchu reached out and pulled a brass chain that lit a single light bulb over my head. The new light revealed the stranger's face. It was drawn in narrow but sturdy lines—a thin face that did not give any feeling of fragility. His eyes were small and black, and did not share the humor of his lips as they pulled back in an angry grin.

"I can't believe she'd pick you ..." He shook his head before removing his hat and hanging it on the doorknob. "God help you."

The light let me see an arrogant man. There was something in his entire bearing that made me know he was prepared to enforce his view of himself.

Blackbeard stepped in front of me as his boss took the one stair down to the uneven floor. The man's movements completely concealed his reasons for bringing me here. He was a poker player of some skill. The fact that he'd allowed me to see his displeasure at all made me wonder how bad a predicament I was in.

He paused, looking at the floor to Blackbeard's left. Then he raised his face to me and let contempt wash over it.

"It's true then." He pointed at his face then mine. "About the clown act." The contempt twisted into a bitter smile. "I heard your name. I know about you. But I thought the clown thing was a joke."

I decided to override the restless spirit being conjured inside me by saying something, "It's no joke."

Part of me contemplated vacating the body and letting Tommy endure what was to come, but I knew that my host's madness was uncontrollable and dangerous. He could get himself killed where, if I was lucky, I might find an opening.

My abductor let real humor appear briefly in his features. "Well, you're wrong there."

He looked at Blackbeard then. "Rub a bit of that makeup off." An evil grin appeared on his features like pain. "Use your fists."

I felt the first two hard hits, and then grayed out. What I mean by that is, I didn't lose consciousness, but my sense of time and reality shifted with each hard punch that Blackbeard fired at my head.

"Stop it," the boss said finally. *Boss* was how I had immediately come to think of him. His voice had a hazy quality but the authority in it remained clear—my head was numb with aftershock. There really wasn't any pain yet. That's the funny thing about a solid punch or a number of them. They don't hurt right away. It's the shock that gets you worked up. And the fact that you know they're going to hurt if you survive.

I looked stupidly around the room. Blackbeard's violence must have bumped the overhead light because the shadows were now moving. Somewhere the boss had found a chair. He set it in front of me and sat. A shimmer of fake concern appeared in his eyes.

"Hurts?" He watched Blackbeard stalk away rubbing makeup off his fists with a handkerchief. "I want to reach you, clean and clear. I don't want to take up any more of my time than I need to."

The boss looked up at Fu Manchu while he rummaged in his jacket pocket. He pulled out the envelope his gangsters had taken from me. My face must have transmitted something more than disorientation and swollen flesh because the boss's eyes clicked to mine.

"You know this envelope, Wildclown?" He held it in both hands and slowly unfolded it. "You want to tell me your story? I already know what's in it. I'm not stupid. But I'd like to hear your story."

"I'm curious too," I said, my lips and jaw slow and heavy. I really needed a cigarette. "I am working from a set of assumptions."

Fu Manchu gave me a little tap on the shoulder. Just enough for me to know he wanted his turn to beat the clown.

"I have heard you refer to a woman." I cleared my throat. "'I can't believe she picked you,' you said. I also very recently met a 'she' who appeared and disappeared from my life in a *unique* that I now recognize as *manipulative* way. Her attention to me was unusual and I should say suspicious, but it put her in proximity to me that would have allowed her to plant something." I noticed my captor's eyes narrow. "Like that envelope."

The boss's hands curled into fists. "Go on ... this is good."

"She had some reason to include me. I don't know what the envelope contains, but I would assume it is evidence of a kind that implicates me in a crime or mystery that involves something you possess." My own eyes narrowed when I started to read things behind the boss's features. "I don't know what that is. The woman's name was Erin Moore. Or that's what she called herself. I believe it was her name since she would have wanted to plant that knowledge on me to corroborate whatever she provided in the envelope and the association that it implies. I think she wanted you to focus your attention on me." I looked at the floor. "She's missing?"

A solid fist caught me behind the left ear and I almost broke free of my host's body. Momentarily I grappled with the madman's soul before he subsided in darkness and pain. "Boss asks the questions!" bellowed Fu Manchu. I braced for another blow but heard the boss.

"That's enough! We'll play out a bit of rope." His voice held real emotion. I pulled myself up, unable to ignore the pain that fired its way up from my shoulders and spine.

The boss said, "She isn't missing. What's your story?"

"Good question," I said. "I wish I knew."

"You better come clean." A slight waver had developed in his tone.

"I'll bet it was easy to find the bar she went to. Where I met her? That bar has never attracted her type. *I'm* almost too good for it. I'll bet you had her followed." I nodded as I watched the boss nod. His eyes burrowed into me.

"What's in the envelope?" I shifted against the ropes deciding it was too early to ask for a little slack. "Erin Moore was your wife."

"Might as well have been," his voice softened when he said it. "We were engaged. I wanted to marry her. But she kept putting things off. You saw her. You don't want to—love—a woman like that and not marry her."

"You know why she put things off?" I knew this was dangerous ground and tensed for a fist in the head.

"She said with statistics being what they were. Especially since the Change," a dark-humored smile shaped his lips. "Said we needed a good engagement period to check see things were right between us. I'm old-fashioned too. So that's okay."

"And things were going well with her." Again I tensed for punishment.

"My work keeps me busy." The boss's whole body flexed as though he wanted to pace but did not want to add to the vulnerability he was already exposing. "And I don't get to see her as much as I like. And so I leave one of the boys here ..." He gestured to Fu Manchu and Blackbeard. "Or others to keep her company. And she didn't like that."

"And recently, she said she was fed up and didn't want any more of it," I said, taking another couple steps onto the thin ice. "She wanted you to trust her."

"No." The boss looked mildly wounded by my statement. "She used to say that. But stopped when I brought her a little bit into the business. I thought that would keep her happy."

I paused knowing that asking him his business was almost guaranteed to get me a beating. He saved me from it.

"I sell diamonds and gems. There's a huge market—wholesale. You know? Authority is pretty strict about moving that stuff in and out of the country. But I have ways of bringing it in from the Old World and Africa without all the paperwork."

Or taxes or duties or proof of ownership, I thought. "And Erin was part of that."

"She helped with some of the manifests for shipments."

"She'd know what was coming and going." My voice dropped as I discovered the thread of something.

"Right." The boss's eyes narrowed. He dropped the last of his cigarette and ground it under his shoe.

"And she was all right with that." I vaguely hoped he would have another smoke.

"Yes. She was—whatever business it is of yours? She liked the job." His smile was inward, satisfied.

"But you still had her followed." I tested my ropes again—still there.

"Like I said. A man wants to marry a woman like that if he's going to feel things for her."

Or *possess her*. I thought. "And you were getting worried ..."

I felt a hard strong hand on my shoulder and I braced for the attack this time from my right. But the boss stopped it with a look. "Let him yak," he told Blackbeard. "Man gets a couple last words we can't fault him." He looked back to me. "I told her we were going to get married this Christmas—asked her ..." He glanced at his watch. "Today. That way, she would have half of everything I own. It's the best deal you know."

"And she didn't jump at the idea. So you had her followed."

"No, I always had her followed." His tone was matter-of-fact.

"Did she get to order product? Did she get to choose when diamonds and gems were purchased by you, your business?"

"She did, yeah." The boss let his first real sliver of doubt escape. "She asked for the responsibility."

"So your boys here follow her as always, but this time they see her enter a seedy bar in the Downings District and sidle up to me and spend an evening in intense and overly friendly conversation." The memory of it gave me a pang. "They see her leave and follow her home. You hear about it, and tell the boys to check me out because this is the night before your wedding day and you're about to share your empire with her which you won't do if there is some clown on the fringe waiting to laugh at you." I braced again but this time even Fu Manchu and Blackbeard were listening to the story. "They quietly reason with me and discover an envelope in my pocket that somehow links me to their boss's betrothed. You read whatever is in the envelope and decide to question me yourself."

This raised the boss's eyebrow.

"I'll bet she arranged for a purchase lately." I glanced at the floor. "She recently acquired for your business a large quantity of small gems—the type that bring a good dollar without raising an alarm. I don't know, maybe some of this stuff is stolen or lost. So, she convinced you lately to make a big buy, some rocks that she just had to purchase so that she would feel good about herself taking on the responsibility. And you want to prove how you feel since you're getting married Christmas day. It's all about trust."

The boss's eyes darkened. "Some stuff from Old Amsterdam. Supposed to be from the Vatican horde. A fortune in small change."

"So here we sit talking," I said. "You have a man following her now?"

"Yeah," said the boss. "I always do."

"If he's lucky, he's lost her." I felt the weight of my assumptions. "If he's not, he's dead."

The boss climbed to his feet. "What are you saying?"

"She decided to look after herself." I shook my head; the numbness was slowly making way for the pain. "Maybe following her was not the best thing, in her mind. But a woman like that, you want to marry them if you're going to feel something ..." I watched a tremor of realization go over him.

"I'll bet these two are your best men." I pointed my chin at Fu Manchu and Blackbeard. "She knew you'd want them with you to talk to me. She slips an envelope into my pocket with something that will cause enough doubt to bring you down here, wherever this is, to personally take part in the questioning. She knows how important Christmas day and marriage is to you, so stages this whole thing the night before."

The boss stepped forward, his limbs stiff. "What are you saying?"

"You better get home or to the office or wherever it is you keep your safe." I glared at him now. Something in these realizations had awakened my sense of injustice. "You're being robbed. If you ever want to see Erin Moore again, or your property you better get moving."

The boss looked up at his men and searched for some sort of help there. Shaking his head he snatched his hat from where it hung on the doorknob. "Leave him tied. We got to get down to the office." He glared at me. "You better be right, or it's going to be a bad Christmas for Wildclown."

The boss had been holding the envelope in one hand the whole time. He crumpled it in a fist and bounced it off my forehead. All three men hurried from the room. I think it was Blackbeard who made sure he grazed my temple with an outstretched elbow. The door closed behind them. The overhead light continued to send wobbly shadows all around me.

# 4
## Christmas Day

So, I got tired of trying to escape. The ropes were tied perfectly—tightening on my wrists the more I struggled. Whoever had bound me, Fu Manchu or Blackbeard, must have been a hell of a Boy Scout in the world long ago before the Change. So instead of escaping, I let my thoughts drift, my body relax as much as possible so that I could detoxify.

I had gulped down a lot of booze the night before and knew that I'd do better with the ropes, with everything, if my breath wasn't coming in wheezing heart-shaking gasps. I'd let things go a bit longer before I put on the final push to save myself. I think I even drifted off to sleep at one point.

I was awake when the red door swung open. I had heard no sound of approaching footsteps; it just opened. The boss stood in the light from the hallway. His hat was low; his overcoat belt was tied tight. I think I saw sweat on his cheeks. He had a knife in his right hand.

I tensed when he stepped into the room—his poise was there, but something looked mildly awkward in his stance.

"Dead," he said cryptically, and then walked behind me. I focused my energy for a final struggle to escape waiting to feel the blade at my throat or in my back.

Instead, I felt the tension on my ropes begin to vibrate and then slacken. The boss was cutting me loose.

"We surprised her and her boyfriend. They were at the office cleaning out the safe." The boss coughed and cleared his throat. "The man I sent to follow her was her boyfriend." Another snap and the rope around my wrists sprung free. The boss gagged or laughed deeply and I felt a *tap-tap* where a pair of small dark red spots appeared on my shoulder. "I say *was* because he's dead."

The boss walked around me to his chair and dropped heavily onto it. "They were filling up a bag. The boys I brought with me went in first, but

Erin's boyfriend, he had one of those auto-shotguns that Authority uses. Blew them in half."

I watched as a growing dark stain traveled over the front of the boss's overcoat. "I shot him." He smiled a minute until the expression melted to sorrow. "But Erin had a gun too ..." His hands fell to his chest. "I was going to marry her."

I stood up and walked over to him. The amount of blood that pooled at his feet told me there was no need to hurry for an ambulance. Something inside him had just let go. He'd die here in the basement, and after a short Blacktime—the period in between life and death—he'd get up and begin a new existence as a slowly desiccating but walking corpse. It would be something but only a shadow of real life.

"I'm sorry," was all I could say. I watched as the life bled out of him, as his eyes slowly glazed.

I looked around the room and found my gun. It was on a small table against the wall behind my chair with a couple of magazines, a lamp and a pen. On my way out I paused, looking down at the envelope.

The paper had been wrung and twisted—the boss had choked the life out of it. I shook my head at Erin's envelope, stepped on it as I left the room. I walked out, up a short stone stair and into an empty warehouse.

Probably near the docks—there were hundreds of them. I let myself out of the building, saw the boss's car, a retro Thunderbird, but decided against borrowing it. There had been a lot of death on the night before Christmas. And if I were lucky, none of it would follow me.

I walked back to my office.

# MURDER IN MOVIELAND

Elmo watched with his trademark slack-lidded stare as I struggled to get the lid off a jar of pickles. I had been grunting and groaning at the job for a full five minutes and was fast approaching the moment that I would pull my gun and start shooting. The whole idea of an impulse buy like this was to brighten up my day, fit something simple into an otherwise work weary life. And here I was close to breaking out in a sweat over a jar of dills.

I stifled a curse and dropped the jar onto the floor of the car after I paused long enough to read the label. In my youthful exuberance to make an impulse purchase I had grabbed a jar of bread and butter pickles instead of the dills I craved. I wouldn't eat a bread and butter pickle if it begged me to.

I looked up at Elmo behind the wheel. A wave of uncertainty passed over his face as he watched the odd climax to my efforts. He looked at the pickle jar, then up at me.

I grimaced, pulled my cigarettes out, and lit one. Hell, I wanted to light two. Half the reason I'd bought the damn pickles was a growing interest in me to do something with my mouth other than crack wise, chew cigarettes and inhale whisky.

I turned back to Elmo, smiled humorlessly then fed a column of smoke into the radio. It was just buzzing now, had slipped into a cataleptic fugue after five frustrating minutes of radio station hunting.

Oily rain slid down the windshield and obscured the world outside. I looked at the distorted view and felt no pang of nostalgia. There was nothing to see out there. We were about eight blocks from the harbor where ancient warehouses crowded. Nearby a movie was being filmed.

It was about two o'clock on Friday afternoon. It was October and the constant rains sometimes turned to slush at night.

I had received a call from Marvin Stewart about an hour before. He was a producer at Killzone Pictures. They were making a horror movie in Greasetown and there'd been some trouble.

The movie, *Open Grave* was based on a runaway bestseller by an obscure author. The author was enjoying his leap into the spotlight because he'd specifically included his position as writer on set in the sale of the movie rights. Well, he had since stopped enjoying it. Apparently all the fun had ended the night before when someone shot him.

He was out of Blacktime, the amnesia like period between life and death that came with the Change, and so I'd be able to talk to him when he returned from Authority HQ where the inspectors in charge were debriefing him. I didn't bother meeting him there.

My work in the Billings Case had started a chain reaction that resulted in the firing of about half the force. I was still averaging two threatening phone calls a day.

Marvin Stewart said to meet him down at the Campbell & Dunn Warehouse. He'd said I'd spot the movie set. I'd know the place. Dingy trailers and recreational vehicles formed a small carbon monoxide belching town in a vast parking lot beside the old red brick structure.

This view was past the sidewalk on my right—just over a rusted chain-link fence. Elmo and I had already seen a pair of strangely costumed corpses hurry by under an umbrella. A burly worker had rushed a tarp-covered cart full of equipment through a gaping door and into the building.

It was at this dim opening that a man in a dark suit appeared waving frantically.

"Maybe that's h-him," said Elmo, anxious to break the monotony of our wait.

"Must be," I said, climbing out of the car into the rain. My cigarette hissed grumpily when exposed to the downpour, and I shifted my head to protect it beneath the brim of my hat. A heavy gray overcoat hid my spotted coverall. I was still soaked from my initial run from the office to the car.

Elmo climbed out of the Chrysler and with a flip of his hand produced an umbrella. He looked at me briefly then kept to himself. We'd already discussed my approach. I wore clown makeup as part of an unspoken deal I made with the man I borrowed my body from and that was enough of an icebreaker for me.

I didn't want to present the scene of Elmo and me hurrying for shelter while struggling to hide from the rain beneath a shared umbrella. I had enough trouble making friends.

I clomped resolutely past the trailer park, lips buckled around my dying cigarette.

Marvin Stewart almost jumped for joy when I walked up and took his hand. His bright blue eyes vibrated over my makeup.

"Wildclown! It *is* true!" He smiled and laughed nervously. His hands leapt to his thin lips. "I'd read about you in the paper. It's perfect!"

He was referring to some articles about my involvement in the Billings case. I didn't like all the interest but I had seen a sharp rise in business since the stories.

"Sure. This is my partner, Elmo," I said. "Did the dead writer get back yet?" The change of subject was my standard refrain.

Marvin Stewart smiled. "You're perfect." His eyes slid over my makeup, he flinched with joy as he looked over Elmo's dead black features, at his rain-dappled, ankle length overcoat. His attention shifted back to me. "We have got to talk ..." He actually giggled, brushed a hand over my upper arm. "You should be in pictures."

I heard Elmo clear his throat nervously.

"Talk to my agent." I glared out into the downpour. "What happened to your writer?"

Stewart squeezed his eyes and mouthed the words: *you're perfect*, before starting. "We started filming *Open Grave* three weeks ago. We've been in pre-production for a year ..." He shrugged his shoulders at the weather and started to walk in away from the doorway. We followed. "The author of the book, Jason Davies, is in seventh-heaven. Do you know he was eating baloney and couldn't afford to do his laundry a week before his book went on the bestseller list? Well, baloney, or whatever it is they make now."

Stewart was referring to the fact that since the Change all dead meat was reanimated. No one knew why, it just was. So most meat-like foods were made out of a paste of something like seaweed and plankton chemically spiced to taste.

Stewart stopped where a massive set of spotlights rested on wheeled platforms. He looked for grease then leaned against a steel upright. "It was a real 'Star is Born' story. And more so, because he was not the real writer in the family."

"What does that mean?" I watched a pair of women in bathing suits walk past. They looked to be pre-Change twenty—and both aware of it. I also noticed that they barely gave me a double take. I was just another oddity in their Movieland world.

"His brother, Steven, was the *up and coming*." Stewart pressed a hand against his breastbone. "But he died in a sailing mishap." He saw my intent expression. "He and Jason were boating enthusiasts and were caught up in a storm—years ago. Steven was lost overboard. Jason, who had been a struggling musician vowed to find a way to memorialize his brother. Make his dreams come true despite the loss."

"So Jason is writer on set?" I added to break the reverie I saw Stewart slipping into.

"Indeed. And yesterday evening he was shot." Stewart's eyes dropped.

"He said he entered his trailer and surprised a burglar."

"And he's been talking about suing you ever since he woke from Blacktime." I torched a fresh cigarette.

Stewart smiled then winced at the plume of smoke. "It has been mentioned. And our lawyers want to investigate it independently of Authority."

"So you can fight it if you have to."

"Exactly," Steward nodded. "Yes."

"Can I see the crime scene while I wait?"

"Certainly," he said and led us toward the makeshift trailer park.

We followed Mr. Stewart past something on a trailer that looked like a blood-covered flying saucer.

## 2
## Crime Scene

I stood opposite Elmo in a cramped trailer about thirty feet long and eight across. On the indoor/outdoor carpeted floor was a bloodstain about a yard wide.

After leading us to the crime scene through a complicated canyon of trailers, Stewart left us to return to wait for Davies at the warehouse. I looked around the modular environment and its particleboard furniture and sneered at its stifling Movieland efficiency.

*Movieland* was what I called anything that had to do with movies.

It wasn't a place it was a state of mind.

It was a world of deals and broken promises.

Where ambition was more important than decency.

Where dreams were made real and where they died.

It was the origin of our ideals and heroes and a memorial to them.

Movieland was politics and religion without accountability.

It was a place you had to smile when they slipped the knife in.

It was a traveling trailer park with money.

Elmo dropped to a knee at the door ran a finger over the sill while I brooded.

"Looks like there's been about a hundred break-ins ..." he said with obvious disappointment.

"Strike one against Killzone Pictures!" I spat.

Elmo clicked his tongue as he locked the door and then easily pushed it open. "Looks like it won't l-lock."

"Strike two," I said kneeling.

My fingers probed a peanut-shaped damp spot on the floor to the right of the bloodstain—a footprint. As I rose I placed a hand on the dark cushion of the chair. It was wet too. "Elmo ... water on this chair."

Elmo came over and touched the cushion with his dead hands, sniffed them, then gave a slight flick of his tongue. "Maybe Davies had a glass of water when he g-got shot."

I looked at the floor—no broken glass, nothing. I pined for the old days when dead people stopped moving. A police chalk line around a body would have been helpful in replaying the scene.

"I want to talk to Davies."

# 3
## Hit and Run

We got there in time for Mr. Davies final death scene. I'm sure he wouldn't have written it that way for himself. I'm sure he wouldn't have written anything that had happened to him in the last twenty-four hours. But as Elmo and I approached the great open door to the warehouse we saw Mr. Stewart gesturing toward the street.

I looked to see a man around six feet in height standing on the far side about a hundred yards from us. He was balanced on the curb and seemed very hesitant in action and uncomfortable in his own skin. That was the way of it for the newly dead. Very disorienting, all fear.

After Blacktime you wake up to find that all the rules had changed. Still even walking death was something. What did he want, a sympathy card? I watched as he stepped off the curb.

There was no time for him to react, because there was barely time for any of us to register what we saw. A large white van with writing on the side of it hit him going about a hundred miles an hour. Mr. Davies slammed into the grill of the vehicle and was carried away. The van went into a complete skid and squealed away from us in a cloud of burning rubber smoke.

"Get the car!" I barked at Elmo as I pulled my gun running beside him toward the street. I hit the sidewalk in time to see the van come to a halt about a quarter mile from us. Its tires screeched, and squawked as it backed up and then roared forward again.

I ran as fast as I could, hoping to get close enough to hit the driver. When I got to within ten yards, I saw the driver's strangely bulbous head look out, and down as he did a final squeal over a dark tangle on the pavement.

I lifted my gun and rattled a few bullets off at him. I think I got the doorframe over his head, but it got his attention. His face centered on me, and then disappeared inside the van. The vehicle tore away.

It was then that I heard the slow *tick-tick* of the Chrysler's engine coming from behind. One look at the greasy and mangled smear on the sidewalk told me that there would be no further questioning of Mr. Davies.

My mind raced from the image of the dead man's hands still twitching. Instead I tore around the Chrysler and leapt into the seat beside Elmo. Ahead we could see the van take a hard right toward the docks.

"Get him, Fatso!" I barked as I pulled the clip for a reload. I glimpsed back to see a horrified crowd of sensitive movie types gathering around what was left of Mr. Davies—the Star is Dead.

I dropped my ammo clip as Elmo took the same hard right toward the docks. The Chrysler's engine roared as we burned the distance between us.

"There he g-goes," muttered Elmo, as the van took another heart-wrenching corner about a half mile ahead of us.

"Get him," I growled, mind racing with adrenaline, hand snatching up the ammo clip and jamming it home.

Elmo locked the wheels and almost flipped the Chrysler as he angled us for entrance to a narrow alley. "I know a w-way," he hissed.

"Get him!" I repeated. I saw Elmo's seat belt was on. I fastened my own.

Elmo's eyes were wide with either concentration or terror as the Chrysler howled down an alley between massive warehouses. We tore over anything in our way—a garbage can appeared and was eaten with a roar.

I looked to my dead partner's face hoping to find some intent or reassurance in his features. Instead I watched his lips move slowly and steadily like he was counting seconds.

A door opened in front of us, it was smashed flat against the wall and flew over the Chrysler's roof—I hoped there wasn't a hand attached.

The car bottomed out as the uneven pavement took a dip and a rise. It bounced off the ground with a shuddering groan.

"Hold on, B-boss!" Elmo cried, and I jammed my feet against the floor.

The alley opened on a cross street. I saw the van appear on our left, heard Elmo shriek then listened as the metal and engines screamed when we briefly locked bumpers. The Chrysler bucked forward and up. The van careened sideways and rolled down the street between the warehouses.

Our momentum carried us forward until we hit the wall across the street on the driver side—hard. My head must have hit the dash, or Elmo or the wheel.

*Transition.*

Next thing I knew, I was floating over Tommy's head.

# 4
## The Chase

If you aren't familiar with my case, I'm a detective who doesn't have a body of his own, apparently. Am I dead? The jury's still out. In order to do my work I have to possess the body of a madman. I call him a madman because of the things he says and because he dresses like a clown. Not a happy clown, a somber one, all in black and white face paint. For clothes he chooses from a selection of coveralls covered with faded spots.

And I'm allowed to possess the body if I follow certain rules. I can't remove the makeup, and I have to be careful how many questions I ask about my host. Both of those things will provoke his suppressed character to surface and expel me like a sneeze. Oh, and severe impacts to the head will do it too.

When I'm disembodied, as I found myself, there is nothing I can do. The only way to re-possess the body was by enlivening a link in Tommy Wildclown's pleasure center. This was often difficult to do when he was angry or hurt.

So, I was cast into the roll of disgruntled balloon floating some feet above Tommy's head dragged along after him by an invisible tether. It's inconvenient and dangerous, and it's not something I put on job applications. For the most part, when I'm in charge I rarely run into trouble with the madman's psyche—and I tend to increase the odds in my favor with liberal applications of alcohol. Tommy usually rests quietly at the back of his mind.

But not now. Tommy screamed and grabbed at his forehead. I saw that a fair bit of blood had already run over his makeup in thin streams. Angrily, he pushed at Elmo who was struggling to get up from under him.

"What's going on?" the clown yelled, shoving his door open. I could see from my vantage point that Elmo was apparently undamaged, though his clothing glittered with safety glass fragments. "Elmo!"

Elmo's legs were tangled under the dash. "He h-hit us," the dead man hissed—mild dismay registering on his features. "In the v-van ..." My partner didn't know about me, and only understood that his boss had erratic moments.

Tommy flicked his head toward the overturned van. It had come to rest in an open alleyway. I could see now that the words *Mamma Parisi's Pizza* were written on the side of it.

"Fucker wrecked our car!" Tommy yelled as he struck blood from his eyes with the back of a hand. "Almost killed me," he muttered as he ran toward the wreck. I was immediately towed along after him.

"Wait!" Elmo called after; his legs appeared to be knotted beneath the wheel. "I'm all s-stuck up."

But I was unable to halt the clown's rage. I could already see that he had not taken the time to retrieve the gun where it had fallen with the impact and that he was likely planning a two-fisted answer to his traffic concerns.

I had been broadcasting mental images of sexual intimacy and disregard since the crash. Tommy was one strange monkey so the dirtier the image the better. But, my attempts to provoke his pleasure center were overcome by his bitter rage. I was worried because I knew there was a great likelihood that the driver of the van had a gun, and he had just used it the other day to kill a writer.

But Tommy rarely knew what went on during my possessions. The clown seemed to have vague impressions, little more. He stomped right up to the overturned van and dropped to his knees. My vantage point afforded me little first hand knowledge but when Tommy got up I knew the driver had already quit the van. Then the clown looked at his hands and rubbed at moisture there. I noticed it too, and then the puddle on the asphalt of what appeared to be water. It pooled around the driver's side window.

"Fucking get me wet too, asshole!" Tommy growled and tore around the van running as fast as he could. I was pulled along after him and was able to see that he was following a pair of bare damp footprints that ran into the trash-strewn alley.

I tried desperately to take over when Tommy rounded a corner and came upon a wide-open sewer. It had two iron doors that opened upward wing-like and the footprints led right to the darkness they revealed. Tommy's mind must have been firing with adrenaline because my attempts to control him were unsuccessful.

I was working so hard because from my invisible vantage point I had already seen the creatures that were lying in wait for him. In the shadow cast by a Dumpster and in the dark alcove beside an air conditioning unit I saw naked people—or rather what had once been people.

Their skins glistened with reflected light and showed an intaglio of blue and greenish veins beneath the waxy skins. They had a bloated, puffy look—an almost translucent quality. Lurking in the shadow were what looked to be two large men—faces swollen beyond recognition or usefulness and a woman—her breasts had engorged to resemble enormous semi-transparent rubber bags full of murky fluid.

When the creatures finally moved, they made squishing noises; but it was not enough warning for Tommy to react. He was bent over peering into the depths of the sewer when they fell on him. There was a massive impact as the saturated forms smashed down on him. Water sprayed in fine droplets as their turgid fists beat on the clown, and Tommy overtaxed was unable to bear his own body weight and those who crashed down on him. As a mass they fell into the sewer.

I was pulled after them at a dizzying speed ...

# 5
## A Trip to the Beach

Tommy's captors were quick to retrieve the unconscious clown from where he floundered in the filthy sewer water. He'd been knocked out by the fall. They hoisted him up. One of the males was injured, rubbed at his rubbery shoulder—ugly crunching sounds came from inside.

"We fix," said his brother. "We fix plenty ..."

"We go." These words came from the female. She was floating in the waist-deep water, legs and arms splayed like a frog's. "We leave the city ... and come no more."

"Where pupil go?" the wounded creature said, as he let his bodyweight be supported by the water. He let out an audible sigh.

"Like we say, pupil go to beach," croaked the uninjured male, his voice was deep and echoing. He wrapped a fist in Tommy's hair dragged him half swimming through the dark water. "We go ..."

"Why take him?" asked the female.

"Him tell about the school. We take him in the water make him pupil. Then him not tell. When him drink big drink, him not tell." The male dragging Tommy hit deeper water. I saw that his body and limbs were better adapted to this mode of transport. His hands and feet spread wide and the flesh between the bones billowed web-like. "We go quickly, others come."

I listened to all this from my vantage point, uncertain of what sort of creature I was looking at. By all appearances they were human, but their bodies were distorted. They continued on like this a few more minutes passing worried phrases back and forth, then fell to silent swimming.

I moved along over top of them, pleased momentarily by the lack of sensory organs as I saw what floating garbage passed in the water. The creatures dragged Tommy like this for almost ten minutes until I saw light appear at the end of the tunnel. All three of them began to kick more strongly, as though the enclosed environment of the sewer had weighed on them all.

When they swam free of the tunnel, I saw at once that it opened onto a refuse covered beach at Greasetown harbor. The rusted hulk of a capsized freighter protected the dirty sand-covered expanse but did not keep the endless stream of flotsam from piling up. The downpour had become a steady rain.

On the beach, squatting toad-like on a coil of rope sat a man thing that I recognized as the driver of the van. The other creatures clambered out of the water dragging Tommy with them. The driver of the van looked up. I saw human emotion flash beneath his distorted features when he saw Tommy's unconscious form.

"Why bring walker?" He rose to his feet and I immediately saw that the flesh of his right thigh had been opened up to the bone from the impact of the crash. It wasn't bleeding. Water or mucous seeped from the torn ligature and muscle. I immediately understood he was a dead man.

"He tell others," said the uninjured male. "We make him swim. Then he happy."

It was then that I detected the first pang of nervous activity from Tommy. He was coming close to consciousness. The female stood near him. She held the clown's other wrist. I saw that her pendulous breasts thumped against Tommy's thigh.

I used that as the starting point for my sexual imagery and Tommy was close enough to consciousness to detect the physical sensations.

# 6
# On the Beach

*Transition.*

I was immediately struck by the smell of the beach, and the boiled cabbage odor coming from my captors. Their frog-like hands were solid but not firm against my arms. With a twist of my legs, I downed the large male and then shoved the female away with an ungentlemanly double hand to the chest. She fell on the beach with a plop of moisture. The sand was hard packed beneath my feet and dimpled by the heavy raindrops that continued to fall.

I snatched up a piece of driftwood in time to meet the driver of the van. He had leapt forward but froze when he saw me ready for the attack.

"Don't do it Steven," I said, watching the creature's eyes flare with recognition. "I don't think you want any more damage." I gestured to his leg. "You're probably in a lot of trouble already."

He squatted—eyebrows wiggling with curiosity. "How?"

"Who else?" I did a slow sideways shuffle to distance myself from the other creatures.

"Who you?" The creature's yellow eyes flashed belligerently.

"I'm Wildclown. A detective." I hefted the piece of driftwood. My ribs hurt like hell. Tommy must have hit something on the way down the sewer.

"Look like clown." He thrust his bottom lip out.

"Why'd you do it?" I growled, suddenly desperately needing a cigarette.

"He deserve!" Steven Davies shrieked, seawater or spittle flying from his mouth.

"Who doesn't?" I growled, casting my glance around, making sure there were no others hiding amongst the refuse. Tommy's captors had retreated to the water and floated there like enormous frogs. "So ..." I turned back to Davies. "Did he kill you before you were lost at sea or did he let you drown?"

"Drown." Davies looked at the sand, dragged a swollen knuckle through it. "No storm like paper say. Push and take the boat away." The creature showed cracked teeth. "He stole my book."

"*Open Grave?*" I watched a sandy tear travel the misshapen cheek.

"He stole my work. *Open Grave* one of many. Of all ..." The creature's fists shook and he punched the ground. "He was jealous of me the younger with talent. I only look up to him."

"So he killed you ..."

"I floated at sea for months, until the others." He gestured to his floating companions. "The Swimmers, they brought me with them. They brought me to their schools and called me pupil." He smiled grotesquely toward his brethren. "There are many Swimmers. All who die at sea are welcome in the schools. But no others. And it is not like land life of walkers. I forgot Jason's jealousy. I was dead at sea, but I had something. There was beauty ..." An ugly memory clenched his features into a horror of waxy folds. "Then I found the magazine. And I read it. Floating in the ocean, fallen from a ship ... I read about Jason's success, about my story and the movie. MY STORY!" A hideous expression outdid the last.

"I had to speak to him." He scowled. "But the land is not safe for Swimmers ... so I look in the ocean sand and find a gun. But I was angry."

I turned when I heard a splashing sound. Elmo was wading through the shallows at the sewer opening. He had my gun in one hand and his .38 in the other, and had them unwaveringly trained on the Swimmers.

"You okay?" he asked. Disdain registered in his voice. One wrist brushed at the lapel of his ruined suit.

"Yes." I gestured at Davies with my club. "Meet Steven Davies."

A quizzical look passed over Elmo's face as he trudged out of the dirty water. Then a wave of realization brought his lips up in a smile and he nodded.

"Who he?" Davies glared threateningly. His distorted features ugly.

"He my partner," I said, starting to speak *Swimmerese.*

"What you do now?" His face became an oversized caricature of worry.

I looked the curious frog-like being up and down. He didn't look like a threat to society. By the look of his mangled leg, he wouldn't be a threat to anything for long.

"Nothing." I saw Elmo's sudden stern look. Even Davies looked amazed. "Why should I?" I continued, dropping the driftwood. I turned my back on Davies and walked over to Elmo. None of the Swimmers moved.

"He m-murdered Jason Davies ..." Elmo whispered, his eyes dark with defiance.

"It ain't pretty, Fatso." I took my pistol from him; thrust it through my pink skipping rope belt. "Jason Davies murdered him first." I brushed my hands against my sodden coat. "It's even."

"But ..." Elmo gestured toward the Swimmer.

"Right and wrong have to be flexible in this world, Elmo." I started to walk up the sandy bank that led through refuse to a high fence and a street. "He killed the man who killed him. His brother already doomed him to pay a greater price than jail." I searched my pockets and pulled out a wet pack of cigarettes. I squeezed them once and tossed them away. "We all pay."

"I g-guess," my dead partner said. I could hear from Elmo's tone that he wasn't convinced. I looked back once as I topped the fence and saw the Swimmer Steven Davies had returned to his seat on the dirty coil of rope.

"We all pay," I said before giving Elmo a hand up the links. I knew there'd be a debate over this one, but I put it aside for the moment to concentrate on making up a story that would get Killzone Pictures to pay for the Chrysler.

# THE GREASETOWN VAMPIRE

It was a night like any other in Greasetown. Dark and wet, the noise of tattered car mufflers vied for dominance with gunshots. The streets were barely alive with the shuffling step of the doomed and the dead. Safe in my little office, I was able to wallow in non-action.

The resulting boredom soon grew to discontent, the discontent to outrage, the outrage to depression, and the depression to an unquenchable thirst. Satisfied with my jury-rigged justification, I picked up my three fingers of whisky and downed it. The heated taste scoured nicotine from my tortured tongue.

Two months had gone by without a case. I had stayed in the habit of possessing Tommy's body every day for the last two weeks to keep in practice. The clown was so bored by the time in between that I found little resistance when taking over.

I envied my partner Elmo at such times. His long-practiced association with death had made him perfectly comfortable with the searing boredom. But he was dead, and whatever animated his corpse was of an electric quality that did not require much amplitude. In fact, there were times he looked more comfortable at rest.

The door to my office opened. Not so much as a knock preceded the action. So deep was I within the creeping tedium I didn't even bother to look up from the contemplation of my empty glass. It would only be Elmo trying to break the monotony with some meaningless trinket of knowledge he'd found in an encyclopedia, newspaper or magazine.

So I was thoroughly surprised when after a heartbeat, an unfamiliar voice spoke to me. It was deep and resonant, and altogether different from my dead partner's whispering squeak.

"Forgive me, Detective Wildclown," it said, its edges colored by a foreign first tongue. "For barging in. I mean no disrespect."

My visitor was tall, maybe six and a half feet and wore an enormous black coat and wide-brimmed hat. His shoulders were almost half again the width of my own. He smiled beneath a thick black moustache; his shadowed eyes flashed in a mysterious but amiable fashion as he pulled his hat from his head and shook loose a tangle of dark locks that cascaded around his bull neck. Nodding rapidly, he bent at the waist in an echo of a courtly bow then extended a hand.

I now realized that some adrenaline impulse had set me on my feet. Always the cool cucumber, I smirked nonchalantly beneath my face paint and reached out to take the hand he offered. I immediately registered my visitor's clammy coolness but chalked it up to the fine film of water that shimmered on his coat like dew. Some of these droplets fell off and stained my desk blotter like spattered blood when we shook. His grip was strong enough to raise my eyebrows.

"No offense," I said, peering past him toward the outer office. It was unlike Elmo to stray from convention or habit, so his allowing a visitor unannounced had me worried. My left hand stayed low near my gun where it hung in a pink skipping rope belt. "Would you excuse me please?" I gestured to the chair opposite my desk. "Have a seat."

I smiled dumbly and moved past my visitor—the sheer mass of him pressed outward and seemed to slow my movements like I was walking into the wind. Continuing to the door that opened onto the waiting room, I peered through the smoky murk. I could see Elmo sunken into the depths of a large leather chair we kept for guests. The dark shadows cast by his reading lamp allowed only a dim blue glow from his eyes and an orange one from his cigarette.

"Taking the night off, eh Fatso?" I frowned, and then saw his concerned mouth snap open. I shook my head then entered my office pulling the door closed behind me. I saw my visitor from an angle that made him look like a hunchbacked hump of muscle wedged into the chair.

"Can I get you a drink?" I lit a cigarette and walked past him feeling his eyes on me all the way. "Whisky?"

"I do not drink liquor," he said and smiled. "It thins the blood."

"Well, here's to thin blood." I hastily poured myself a drink and upended it.

"Forgive the intrusion." My guest's eyes flared potently. "But I could not delay. In truth, I debated coming to you until the very moment I stood at your curbside. When the decision was made I had to act."

"Nice to get the vote of confidence." My cigarette glowed mutely as I dropped into my chair.

"I mean no offense." He looked down at the large powerful hands that wrestled like demi-gods in his lap. "I debated this action only because I am capable of taking care of my own problems. I only wish to remain within the confines of our laws and would like to keep my reputation unsullied."

"Oh." I smoked. "That's different. Why don't we begin with introductions then your problem?"

"Of course." He nodded slowly. "Introductions first." From the cramped position of his chair, he did the little half bow again. "Forgive me for not telephoning ahead and arranging the appointment. I understand my sudden appearance must have alarmed you. My name is Gregor Tzukar—a businessman, I will tell you no more than that. I come to you with a problem that you will undoubtedly find undeserving of my hesitation and of your formidable abilities of succor."

"Okay," I said, not passing up the opportunity for some verbal fencing.

"A group of forever youths has taken possession of one of my properties and I would like to hire you to deliver an eviction notice to them. No more than that." Tzukar reached into his heavy overcoat and drew out a neatly folded paper. He leaned forward, tossed it on the desk. "You will find it in order."

"Why don't you just tack it up? You look like you can take care yourself." I picked up the eviction notice. "As I understand it, once it's in place, you can call Authority housing in."

"Of course, I am quite capable." His eyes smoldered suggestively. "Under normal circumstances I would deliver it myself." He went silent a moment, gauging his next statement. "But, I have come to value life and too much enjoy the luxuries afforded by my wealth to risk such an altercation personally." His hands started wrestling in his lap again. "I recently returned to the continent after spending an extended period of time at properties I own in the Old Country. For two decades have I been away, and upon my return attempted to gain entrance to a mansion I own in Greasetown. The neighborhood has declined during my absence and is now called a Downings District." My visitor smiled without humor. "But I found squatters had taken up residence there."

"You said forever youths ..." I was interested now. All that talk about Old Country just had to grab my curiosity. I also knew that forever youths—teens I called them—were different from the forever children.

Forever children: basically kids who ceased to age after the Change but ranged from five to thirteen years had been rounded up by Authority long ago or hidden by loved ones. Forever teens had become permanent adolescents after the Change. Their hormone-charged passions made them eternally dangerous and impetuous. They were avoided by all but the sex and drug trades.

"Yes," Tzukar breathed. "Two greeted me at the doors of my property and offered every manner of insult and threat. I am also certain I heard the sound of weapons being readied for use—*cocked* I think you say. My time with the Serbian militia in the 1990s encouraged that conclusion."

"I'll put the notice up for two hundred dollars." I stood, watching my guest intently.

"Two hundred then." Tzukar rose to his feet and drew a large wallet from his coat. He put a pair of hundreds on the desk. "And two hundred more if you complete this tonight." Tzukar pulled another pair of bills from his wallet, smiled and then slid them back into place. "Upon completion."

I picked the eviction notice up and grimaced at the address.

# 2
# Downings District

"But Boss, I didn't h-hear nobody-no one knocking, not nothing. I wasn't s-sleeping. Or day dreaming." Elmo stammered, beside himself with professional embarrassment. He was addled enough to start slipping in and out of proper English—hard to do with a dead mouth. "I ain't drunk or c-crazy. He didn't come through any door I was guarding."

"Okay, Fatso," I drawled around a cigarette. The discussion had gone on too long all ready. I trusted my partner's perceptions, and he had clearly experienced some gap in memory. I remembered his look of horror and shock when I had ushered Tzukar out of the office some hour and a half before.

"God help us," I said to change the subject. I nodded my head at the dead speed freaks that crouched away from the drizzle in the doorway of a coffee shop. Downings District had been an older section of Greasetown in need of some improvement when the Change came and it had gone downhill ever since.

The newly risen dead had made it their refuge after the first heady years of their attempted reintegration failed. Criminals called it home as well. Their clients and prey soon followed. I stayed clear of Downings as much as possible—it was just too easy to die there.

"That way." I pointed to an interchange that would take us to the center of Downings where the oldest buildings and neighborhoods could be found. We passed a group of people dead and living. They stood in the street watching a ten-story building burn. Eager interest shone in many eyes with the departing boredom.

Distantly, I heard sirens. Elmo slowed the car as we passed. He drove a reconditioned pre-Change Chrysler that had long since lost its hood ornaments and chromium nametags. It was as big as a tank.

In twenty minutes, the interchange took us to a gray neighborhood of heavy looking buildings with graffiti covered walls and rain-scarred roofs and buttresses. The road was pitted and in places more gravel than asphalt.

The Tzukar Mansion looked like a decrepit castle. It appeared at first glance to be made of solid sheets of granite or concrete rising about three stories. And its gothic style allowed for narrow lancet windows, all of them barred, that would give vandals and thieves a difficult time in entering.

The front door, tall iron bound timbered affairs opened onto the potholed street. A tall dead tree stood some ten feet from them, and its twisted stance, remaining branches reaching outward gave it a look of torment and had me unconsciously repositioning my gun.

The building itself must have had many rooms. The structure had a massive quality that suggested expanses within. Its design whispered darkness and secrets. The Tzukar Mansion appeared to have been built in a time before the neighborhoods crowding it existed. So the ten-foot stone wall that swept away from the sides and rounded a sheltered back yard must have originally been designed to keep animals and vagrants at a distance.

I pulled my fedora low and raised my collar. I slipped a box of nails into my overcoat pocket, and then snatched up the eviction notice and hammer. "It's got to be on the building, right?" I scanned the stone structure. "Nailed to the door I guess." Elmo's eyes were full of concern.

"It does seem a little too easy ..." I nodded. "Let's just do it quick."

I steamed out of the car into a new onslaught of rain. It spattered wetly on the glistening pavement—grew heavy on the shoulders of my overcoat. Elmo exited and rounded the car. His hands were deep in his pockets when he joined me. I knew one of them was wrapped around a .38 caliber snub-nose.

"Easy," I repeated as though it was a prayer to the gods-of-just-please-for-once-let-something-be-easy.

"Stay back and keep me covered," I told Elmo as we walked to the tall wooden doors. I pulled out the eviction notice. Elmo stood back about eight feet, his stance strangely livid.

Four nails—one hundred dollars each. Doesn't get easier than that.

And I had a hard time believing it until the third nail was in and home—my spirits actually lifted then, became downright optimistic. My hammer strokes had boomed against the mansion's dark interior and nothing bad had happened. But as I fumbled for the last one-hundred-dollar nail, my skepticism was rewarded when I heard a scream.

A woman's scream. And it wasn't coming from the building's cavernous depths where I had been expecting trouble but from my left, and outside. Again the scream.

I looked at the notice's final free corner. It had begun to flap and snap against the door in the wet, heavy wind. I turned to Elmo. He had the look on his face. It said: *Boss is going to get into it. No such thing as easy money.*

I slipped my hammer into a cavernous overcoat pocket and gestured for Elmo. When he drew near I nodded to the wall. "In your opinion, did you hear that come from over the wall?"

"Yes," he said, with professional exactitude. Elmo was anxious to put the questions about his lapse in sentry duty behind him.

"That's what I thought." I looked at the door, and saw that if I were to have a bit of help, I could get a boot on the second iron hinge and make a lunge for the top of the wall that attached itself to the building about ten feet up. I looked at Elmo. "I'm just going to have a look." There was another scream.

Elmo quickly braced his back against the wall, and made a stirrup of his hands. I set a boot there and then one atop the hinge. When I reached the top of the wall, I saw an open muddy courtyard within. There was some kind of a shed or garage in back.

I watched as two medium-sized men in long coats dragged a struggling woman out of it and toward the rear of the mansion. She made an attempt to run, and was knocked unconscious by one of her captors. They dragged her in.

I heaved my rain-sodden weight against the top of the wall and pulled. I had to thank my host, Tommy's, natural genetics for giving him a consistent muscle tone that our worst excesses refused to completely degrade. I was panting and felt sweat break from beneath my makeup when I finally straddled the top. Beneath me, Elmo stared up like disappointment incarnate.

"I'm going to have a look." I gestured past the wall. "Looks like a kidnapping—something."

Elmo lifted his hands waiting for me to pull him up. It wouldn't have been hard. The desiccated state of his body had him under a hundred pounds. But I stopped him.

"You go get Authority," I kept talking before he could protest. "I need you to do that Fatso. It's a kidnapping. Tell them that." I knew he would have a hard time getting Authority to listen to him. Generally, the dead were considered low class citizens by the living.

Elmo nodded and then backed away toward the car. I wouldn't need to tell him to hide the gun. Authority didn't like dead men having them.

I swung my leg over and then slowly, gingerly attempted to lower myself to a bare tree branch. There was a long line of dead bushes that grew around the inner wall of the yard. The branch broke when I set my weight on it, but I had expected as much and used it only to slow my descent. My combat boots sank ankle deep into the mud. I could tell from its dark color, texture and quality that the gardens had once been a well-tended place.

There was a loud metallic bang, then another. It came from the distant end of the mansion, perhaps one hundred feet from me behind another great profusion of dead or dying shrubbery. I pulled my .44 automatic and ran toward the sound.

The grounds were soft and muddy from the years of rain and I had to watch my step to keep from being mired. I reached the corner of the building, my lungs clogging on old cigarettes, and whipped my head around.

It was dark; the streetlight barely gave the area more than a dim blue glow. I saw low stone walls that bordered a short stairway to the basement.

Gun out and positioned, I hurried over to count down the twelve steps to an eight by four iron door. I knew when I first set a palm against it that it would be locked. A quick examination showed me that a bazooka would have trouble opening it.

I ran back up the stairs and began a quick search of the building's foundation. I immediately saw dim slivers of light slicing through the tangled shrubs that grew around the building's base.

I struggled past the least of these barriers and peered through the foggy window. Inside there must have been ten lamps flickering in a ring of floor sconces and hundreds of candles. They illuminated an open space maybe twenty feet on a side. In the center of this was a large wooden box eight-feet-long, four-feet square on the end—coffin-like in structure. I saw others like it in the shadows.

What made this one in the center different was the nude blonde woman struggling on it. She had been chained in place and didn't seem to like it. Blood trickled from one temple, and I saw that it mingled with the dark roots that grew around her ear. She did not look well, and had the scrawny, unhealthy appearance of someone who had been living on the streets.

I was just saying to myself that all I had to do was wait for Elmo and Authority to return when three individuals came out of the darkness on the blonde's right. They were cloaked in long black robes, and moved as though they were enjoying some kind of archaic tempo driven rite. They moved forward slowly, with heads bobbing until they crowded around the chained figure.

The captive screamed, but the building's thick stone walls muffled the sound.

One figure had taken up position at her head, and there was one looming to either side of her. I was still convincing myself to wait when the figure at her head raised its arms and the heavy black material fell away to reveal a long sharp knife. This came down and softly stroked a light line of blood from the woman's breastbone.

"Damn!" I growled, and looked at the window: about two feet wide by one foot high. I'd fit, but not quickly.

"Damn!" I gave the old glass an elbow, and it burst inward. The woman's screams now pealed insanely in the darkness.

"God Damn!" I growled again, as I pushed myself recklessly forward.

One hand on my gun, I had to keep my left cocked to turn my descent or I'd break my neck. I heard a harsh call, then another. I didn't have time to look or think.

I snagged the corner of the window and swung my legs out and down.

"Damn!" I barked, eyes peering into the darkness as I hung precariously. The woman was still chained in place. The light seemed lower. I cast about in the shadow for the others. Then the muddy window ledge let me down.

I hit the ground off balance and crashed into one of the large wooden boxes. As I staggered to my feet the first of the black-cloaked figures was on me.